Tucklebinnie Goes Travelling

First Published in Great Britain 2017 by Mirador Publishing

Copyright © 2017 by Tom Lindsay
Artwork Copyright © 2017 by Paddy Allen

First edition: 2017

Any reference to real names and places are purely fictional and are constructs of the author. Any offence the references produce is unintentional and in no way reflects the reality of any locations or people involved.

A copy of this work is available through the British Library.

ISBN: 978-1-912192-71-7

Mirador Publishing
10 Greenbrook Terrace
Taunton
Somerset
UK
TA1 1UT

Tucklebinnie Goes Travelling

Tom Lindsay
and
Paddy Allen

CHAPTER 1
A (sort-of) Wizard and Feathered Felons

On the day that this story starts, Tucklebinnie was in his cellar, dealing with a bad-tempered batch of beer which just didn't want to be bottled. Tucklebinnie looked a bit like a wizard probably ought to look because he was one. Sometimes. Mostly when he remembered to be a wizard, or someone needed doing whatever it is that wizards do. Otherwise, he collected stamps, made beer in his cellar, which he sold to passers-by on hot days, and fixed bits and pieces for everyone in the village, and in nearby villages, when whatever the bits were needed repair.

Tucklebinnie was in his cellar, dealing with a bad-tempered batch of beer which just didn't want to be bottled...

He was nearly tall but a bit scraggly around the edges, his beard was a place where small birds could nest if they were tired, or afraid, and as for his clothes, well… He wore a robe, with lots and lots of pockets, with lots and lots of useful things in them, only he could never seem to find them when they were needed. He also had a pointy hat, but he couldn't wear it indoors, because the rooms in his cottage were a bit low. His trousers were held up by some string which had arrived on the outside of a parcel and the bottoms of the trouser legs nearly always had bicycle clips, fixed just above the tops of his great big clumpy boots. He did not have a cat, or a dog, or a magpie, but he had made friends with Isaac, the great-crested newt who lived in Tucklebinnie's garden, in the pond near the well.

"Drat and blast," he said, as the beer resisted his attempts at bottling. Tucklebinnie didn't swear - he didn't need to - because he'd picked up so many excellent words on his travels that he could always find one or two which suited the occasion perfectly and anyway, his mum had said swearing just showed you had no imagination.

…he had made friends with Isaac, the great crested newt who lived in Tucklebinnie's garden, in the pond near the well….

"Listen, you recalcitrant brew, you," he continued. "You've spent the last two weeks burbling away here in this lovely cool cellar, now it's time to go and meet people! Stop swishing about in the barrel and just hop into these nice green bottles."

Quite why anyone would talk to beer is a bit of a mystery, but such are the ways of wizards. In any case, the beer refused to listen to him and sulked in its barrel as he tried to scoop some out in a jug and pour it into the bottles. Sometimes this is easy to do, but on other days, like this one, the beer seemed to deliberately overflow the filling funnel, or to make so many bubbles and foam that it was impossible to see how much (or how little) was actually in each bottle. Just as Tucklebinnie was about to use some *very* colourful foreign phrases, he heard the 'clang, clang' of the horseshoe and bucket which was his doorbell. Giving the beer an 'I'll sort you out just now' look, he shambled up the rickety stairs to his hallway.

"Just a moment," he called out, glancing in the hallway mirror to make sure that he was presentable. By any normal standards he wasn't, but by his standards he was fine and at least he had remembered to put on his second-best shirt and third-best trousers and he had cleaned his teeth that morning after breakfast. He opened the front door, but it seemed as if no-one was there. He looked down.

"Hello, George," he said. Somewhere about knee-level stood his best friend, George the Magical Gnome, getting ready to give the chain, to which the doorbell was attached, another pull.

"Come in, come in," said Tucklebinnie. "Go through to the sitting room (actually there was only the choice of the sitting room or the kitchen) and grab yourself a seat. I'll just put the kettle on. Tell me what's up in a moment."

'Hello, George,' he said. Down about knee level...George, the magical gnome getting ready to give the chain.. another pull.

George, who was in the regulation gnome uniform of a floppy cap, red jacket, green leggings, a big wide leather belt with pouches attached and some very fine pointy boots, did as he was asked and hopped up into Tucklebinnie's second-most comfortable chair. It had seen better days, that was for sure, but despite the stuffing sticking out of the arms and the odd earwig and beetle crawling about, it was good to sit in.

"Right then," said Tucklebinnie. "What brings you here? I thought you were supposed to be off to see your cousin Bert for a day or so - you know; the one that stays near the Pointy Mountains?"

"I was," said George. "I set off this morning, early, and then I remembered I'd said to Bert that I would bring him some of my purple carrot seeds but I'd left those in my greenhouse, so I had to go back. Just as I reached my gnome-home, two big birds flew over me, blocking out the sun, and wouldn't you know it, they landed in my garden and started to rootle about and dig up my carrots with their big yellow beaks!"

"Let me guess," said Tucklebinnie. "They'd be about the size of one-and-a-bit a someone about your size, they'd have orange legs and their wings would be a grotty green colour?"

George looked at the wizard, amazed. "How'd you know that?" he asked.

"I've had to deal with these pests before," said Tucklebinnie. "They're Flugglebirds. They're not that rare, but they generally live

Flugglebirds ... They'd be about the size of one-and-a-bit of someone your size, they'd have orange legs and their wings would be a grotty green colour?

somewhere around the Pointy Mountains. Their favourite food is the sweet-and-sour parsnips (and the occasional sugar-beet plants) which grow near the Noisy River. They do like carrots, a bit, but parsnips are sweeter and as for sugar-beet, well…

"They're a bit thick," he went on. "Absolutely no sense of direction whatsoever, so if they get lost in a big storm or because a strong wind blows them sideways, they just fly about aimlessly, looking for food. The green tops of purple carrots look a bit like parsnips, so I expect they were hungry, saw your garden and thought 'Lunchtime!'"

"That's all very well," said George. "But right now, they're snoozing in my garden, and when they wake up, if they carry on eating my carrots, I'll have none left to see me through the winter. D'you have any idea what I should do?"

Tucklebinnie didn't reply immediately, but went through to the kitchen, where the kettle had begun to boil, and reappeared in a few minutes with two cups of tea and a plateful of 'Binnie Biscuits' (just shortbread really, made with extra butter).

After George had had a slurp or two of tea, and was on biscuit number three (who's counting, anyway?) Tucklebinnie said that he'd had an idea.

"You were going to see Bert, right? So why don't we just capture these pesky pests and take them with us, then find out where they've been seen lately around the Pointy Mountains and let them go?"

"What's this 'we'?" asked George. "Are you going to come with me?"

"Well," said Tucklebinnie. "I've just got to have a word with my latest batch of beer -don't ask - and then I haven't got anything important to do for a few days, so I wouldn't mind seeing Bert again. I haven't been out his way for a good while and my boots need some exercise. Is that fine with you?"

"I certainly don't need Flugglebirds messing about with my carrots," said George. "If they're so thick they can't find their own way home, I'd better help them and yes, Bert would like to see you, I know, so let's get things sorted."

"Right," said Tucklebinnie. "You nip off home and keep those pests sleepy; just bung a carrot or two in their general direction if they wake up - and I'll be along as soon as I have everything in order here."

An hour or so later, the beer having been persuaded into bottles and put away in a nice dark corner of the cellar where it could snooze quietly, Tucklebinnie gathered up his travelling kit into a tattered rucksack.

"Compass - check! Book of spells - check! Socks and underpants - check! Tin of treacle - check! Winklepicker knife, spoon and screwdriver - check! Rucksack - check! Snorkel - check! Hankies - check! Goblin declogger - check! Soap and toothpaste - check! Hat - check!"

Umm, he thought to himself. *I suppose I'd better take Bert a present. Stuffed alligator? No - too big. Ah, I know, I'll take him a super-strength pogo-stick, just right for leaping over pesky boulders in the mountains - after all, he's just a little chap.*

"One more thing - a Flugglebird trap!" he said to the world at large.

Outside the cottage, in a rickety shed, Tucklebinnie dug around, disturbing snoozing spiders, weary woodlice and a considerably cross centipede, until he found what he wanted. It was like a wheelbarrow, with two handles and a big front wheel, but it had a large metal cage on the top with containers for water and food inside and a sneaky wooden walkway which led from ground-level to the door of the trap. He found some nice dry straw in a string net inside the shed and placed a few handfuls on the floor of the trap. There was room around the outside of the cage for the rucksack and a few days' worth of bread, cheese and water and the pogo-stick. As a special concession to George, Tucklebinnie magicked up a small seat at the front, in case he got tired of walking. Well, there's no point in being a wizard if you can't help your friends, is there? Particularly if their legs are much, much shorter than yours.

Tucklebinnie closed the door of his cottage, said a spell to keep out anyone with less-than-honest intentions (you try convincing the local policeman that the flashing sign on the back of your jacket which says 'I'm a failed burglar' or 'Stolen from Tucklebinnie' is just a friendly joke) and set off to meet George on the other side of the village, pushing the FluggleTrap and his luggage.

George had left his rucksack outside the front door and was busy keeping watch on the dozy and rather full of carrot Fluggle birds who were resting and burping in the shade of the conker tree

George's home was a neat little wooden house - a gnome-home - in a sort-of mushroom shape, where the thatched roof was much bigger than the building over which it hung. George had left his rucksack outside the front door and was busy keeping watch on the dozy and rather-full-of-carrot Flugglebirds who were resting and burping in the shade of the conker tree in George's vegetable garden.

"Anything new happening, George?" he asked, as he parked the wheeled cage next to George, sitting on a tree-stump with an armful of carrots, looking grumpy.

"Those pestiferous pointy-beaked parrots, or whatever they are, are messing up my vegetable garden," said George. "They've moved on from the carrots to my beautiful beetroot. How'm I going to save my vegetables?"

"Ah," said Tucklebinnie. "Now just pay attention here; give me a couple of carrots, please."

He delved into his rucksack and brought out the tin of treacle, which he opened quite carefully. I don't know if you've ever been attacked by some treacle trying not to escape from a tin, but it's a sticky, tricky business. Fortunately, Tucklebinnie's Uncle Humphrey, on his dad's side of the family, was a treacle-bender by profession and had taught the fledgling wizard a trick or two about unleashing wild treacle on the world. The best thing is to open the tin slowly and gently, so the treacle doesn't get upset by the sudden daylight and harden like cement.

In the shade provided by his robe, Tucklebinnie gently coaxed a spoonful or so of the sticky liquid onto each of the carrots, where it settled down, then he closed the tin-lid and replaced it in his rucksack. He then turned the Flugglebird trap around so the door end of the cage was in line with the little path which led out of George's garden. He placed one treacly carrot in the cage, leaving the door open and lowering a small ramp to the ground. Taking the other treacly carrot in one hand, he said, "Right, watch this."

He slowly walked up the path towards the conker tree, gently waving the carrot in front of him, just enough so the slight breeze carried the scent of treacle and carrot towards the recumbent avian nuisances. Now, treacle-and-carrot may not be your favourite combination of tastes, but for Flugglebirds, it's just the best thing, ever. A bit like a super-parsnip.

The Flugglebirds kept coming, their beady eyes glued to this tantalising morsel which was just, ever so just, out of reach of their beaks...

The feathered felons snuffled a bit in their dozy state, then their eyes opened wide and Tucklebinnie could almost see their thought-bubbles. "Sweeties (or whatever the word is in Fluggle), sweeties, SWEETIES!" They staggered up, burping gently, and headed towards Tucklebinnie, who slowly moved backwards towards where George was sitting. As he retreated, Tucklebinnie kept wafting the carrot and the Flugglebirds kept coming, their beady eyes glued to this tantalising morsel which was just, ever so just, out of reach of their beaks. Tucklebinnie moved carefully behind the trap and now the treacle-and-carrot scent was doubly strong, owing to the other carrot he'd left in the trap. The Flugglebirds simply followed the scent, up the ramp, not noticing the slight change in slope. As soon as they were inside, squabbling over the second carrot, Tucklebinnie rushed around to the open door and closed it, throwing the first carrot inside. The birds didn't notice the door closing as they pecked and slurped at the carrots.

"That's it, George," said Tucklebinnie. "We'd better take a few carrots with us for the journey, but I'll bet the pests have a good long sleep now."

"Just give me a little while to tidy up the mess they've made," said George, who unlocked his garden shed and took out a rake and a fork. George, who was by far the best gardener in the district, did not use magic to help grow mammoth marrows, colossal cabbages or any of his other vegetables. Instead, he simply spent a lot of time weeding, watering and persuading garden pests to go somewhere else. After quite a few minutes' work repairing the damage caused to his vegetable beds, George cleaned the tools and replaced them, locked the shed, put his rucksack next to Tucklebinnie's and was ready.

"Off we go," said Tucklebinnie. "I do hope Bert's pantry is well-stocked!"

CHAPTER 2
Taking the Flugglebirds home

It wasn't that far to Bert's home, as a Flugglebird might fly, but on the rather wiggly road which the two friends had to follow (particularly as Tucklebinnie was happy to chat to passers-by) it took about five hours.

To the West the travellers could see the foothills of the Pointy Mountains... to th South the Noisy River.. to the North-West.. the fringes of the Fantastic Forest where the rhubarb was ripening

Truthfully, Tucklebinnie's chatting was just to give George a rest every so often - he wouldn't sit on the seat because he was worried that Tucklebinnie's arms would get very tired - so he trotted alongside the wheel-cage. The Flugglebirds had demolished the treacly carrots quite quickly and had then given into the very pleasant feeling of a gentle swaying, with full tums, which being in the cage imparted. They fell asleep. However, they also snored quite a bit, which was a little off-putting.

"George," said Tucklebinnie. "Remind me what Bert does for a living, would you, please?"

"He's got a couple of jobs, actually, depending on the season," said George. "Some of the year, he's a brassica wrangler - you know, making sure the broccoli plants don't stray too far, rounding up the

In the early summer Bert
is a rhubarjack...

sprouts before Christmas, counting the cabbages and keeping an eye on the kale - but quite honestly he's fed up with green vegetables, so that's why I'm taking him the purple carrot seeds. For a bit of variety."

George continued. "In the early summer, he's a rhubarjack for a couple of months or so."

"A what?" spluttered Tucklebinnie.

"A rhubarjack," said George. "Someone who cuts down trees is a *lumberjack*, correct? Not a *treejack*, not a *log lopper*, not a *shrub shortener*, but a *lumberjack*. Bert looks after some of the big rhubarb forests near his home and when the rhubarb's ready to harvest, he cuts the stalks. So, he's a *rhubarjack*. Look, rhubarb might not be that big for you non-gnomes, but for us, some of those big clumps block out the sun."

"Oh," said Tucklebinnie. "That's silly of me to forget. I thought he had something to do with treacle…"

"Ssshh," said George, looking around. "We don't talk about that. Treacle mining is a bit of a sore subject in these parts. I'll tell you more when we're behind some walls, not out here where you don't know who might be listening," he said, pointing with his thumb at the snoring and burping birds.

As they approached the little village where Bert lived, they could see, to the west, the foothills of the Pointy Mountains beginning to appear out of the summery haze; to the south, the Noisy River was swinging towards them in a great bend and just visible to the north-west were the fringes of the Fantastic Forest, where the rhubarb was ripening in sunny dells.

"Not far to go," said George. "I hope Bert's got the kettle on. I could really do with a cup of tea and a sticky bun!"

"Hello, George," said Bert, hopping from one foot to the other as the travellers approached. "You've brought that wacky wizard with you, I see. And what's that he's pushing?"

"It's a Flugglebird trap," said George. "I was just about to set off, when these two ravenous ravens, or whatever they are, started ruining my carrot patch. Luckily, Tucklebinnie knows about these pests and he caught them. Because they live over this way, we thought we'd bring them near to their home and point them in the right direction when they've finished digesting my carrots! Who knows where they'd have

Bert's house, or as it was known by his neighbours, Bert's Barn, was a bit of a ramshackle building..

ended up if we left them in my vegetable patch. Or whether I'd have any vegetables left!"

"Oh well," said Bert. "If we take them to the edge of the forest, they'll soon get their bearings.

"Hello, TeeBee," he continued. "It's a while since I last saw you - when we demolished all those doughnuts on George's last birthday, if you remember - how're you keeping?"

"I'm fine, Bert, thanks," said Tucklebinnie. "Just thought I'd give George a bit of a hand with these winged wayfarers and then perhaps do a little sightseeing."

"Excellent," said Bert. "Just park the trap in the shade here - I'll get some fresh water for those dozy dodos - then come on into the house."

Bert's house, or as it was affectionately known by his neighbours, 'Bert's Barn', was a bit of a ramshackle building. Built of different sorts of wood, it had gnome-size doors set into bigger, human-sized doors at the front and back. The windows were a little bit wonky and the rooms inside were all different sizes, particularly the heights of the ceilings, so that humans could feel comfortable in at least two of them. It seemed to Tucklebinnie, who hadn't been there before, that the house had sort-of grown by itself, over time, to accommodate guests of wildly different proportions.

What was really interesting was the workshop at the back of the house, where Bert stored his various bits of equipment. He was keen to show these off to Tucklebinnie, and demonstrated how the rhubarb loppers lopped, how the gooseberry grippers gathered the berries and how the brassica binoculars could automatically spot a bolting broccoli plant. There was some other equipment under a dusty old sheet which Tucklebinnie was keen to have a look at but Bert said, "Not now - let's keep that for later!"

While Bert had been showing off, George had boiled the kettle in the kitchen, found some ordinary tea-bags - not a rhubarb-flavoured variety - and had made a pot of tea for the three companions. Bert rootled about the pantry and emerged with, surprise, surprise, some rhubarb tarts, half a chocolate cake and some custard cream biscuits, which tasted only slightly of rhubarb. Bert and the two travellers refreshed themselves and then, because it was getting a bit late in the afternoon, he suggested that it was time to let the Flugglebirds find their way home.

"Follow me," said Bert, setting off on a quite well-used track which went in the general direction of the Fantastic Forest.

Tucklebinnie lifted the FluggleTrap handles and pushed the contraption after Bert, up a slight slope and then on some flattish ground for about a mile to a spot near a stream where the Pointy Mountains could be seen in the distance. He lowered the handles so the ramp leading to the cage could be let down to the ground. George climbed up and opened the front door of the cage. Inside, the by-now-wide-awake feathered twosome squawked a bit and tripped over their feet, but with a bit of vocal encouragement from George, and with Bert wafting a carrot in the background, they eventually staggered down the ramp.

Bert understood and could speak a smattering of the Fluggle language so he said, "Right, you two. Listen up. If you can get airborne here, head that way," he said, pointing west.

"Your families are about fifteen minutes flapping time away, so don't bother looking for food, just get on home!"

The birds looked at one another and it was obvious they were thinking, well, as much as birds think, *Why's this bald* (Bert had no feathers, so he was, to them, bald) *beakless biped speaking our language? What's he saying?*

Flugglebirds are not noted for being the smartest of their species;

however, they got the message, eventually, and lolloped along the open ground until they gained flying speed. Fortunately, a faint scent of parsnip had been carried on the breeze and this guided them in the right direction.

"Thank goodness," said George. "Perhaps my garden will recover from that avian attack - provided those two, or their friends, don't get lost again!"

"Don't worry, George," said Bert. "They're youngsters and probably just lost their way; Flugglebirds generally know that if they reach the Fantastic Forest they should turn around, otherwise 'No Parsnip Time' will come along quickly. They're greedy creatures, so are guided by their tums."

"Talking of tums," said Tucklebinnie. "It's been a bit of a long day, and nice though that little snack was earlier, my tum is saying 'FOOOOD'."

"Come on then," said Bert cheerily. "Let's go and find out what tasty morsels live in my pantry. Just as well I stocked up the other day, seeing I've now got two visitors! And one's not even a gnome."

CHAPTER 3
The Dynamic Drill

Back at the 'Barn', Bert suggested that the visitors might like to help make a fire outside in a rather sheltered area where there were two sets of wooden seats nestled against a grassy bank. Taller people could sit on the upper set and shorter people on the lower one, but everyone could enjoy the fire and if a few crumbs of food happened to fall to the ground, well, the local bugs, mice and other small wildlife could have a bit of a feast.

Bert suggested that the visitors might like to help make a fire outside, in a rather sheltered area

Bert's pantry proved to be well-stocked indeed, and soon the visitors - and Bert - were tucking into mushroom pies, cheese and onion flans, pickled onions, fresh lettuce with home-made mayonnaise, and juicy tomatoes. Yet more rhubarb tarts and some very fancy pastry concoctions appeared for afters. Everything was washed down with some rather delicious beer, although a little hint of rhubarb might just be noticed by the discerning drinker. Gnomes, in this part of the world, tended to be more vegetarian than not; Tucklebinnie, who did eat meat quite frequently didn't mind, because the food was tasty and - even better - there was lots of it.

"D'you bake these pies and whatnot yourself, Bert?" asked Tucklebinnie, his teeth getting to grips with a particularly piquant pickled onion.

Bert blushed... 'My girlfriend, Bluebell... knew George was coming so she came over for the afternoon a couple of days ago and helped me bake'

Bert blushed a bit and said, "Not exactly. My girlfriend, Bluebell, who lives just up the road with her mum and dad, knew George was going to visit so she came over for the afternoon a few days ago and helped me bake. She's better than me at the fancy bits of pastry. She's had to go to Port 'na Storm to see her granny, so I don't know if you'll meet her on this visit."

George looked at his cousin. "Well, that's a nice bit of news, Bert; what does Bluebell do?"

"She's an apprentice gooseberry gatherer," said Bert. "S'not a job for just anyone, you know. Those gooseberry bushes have some rather nasty spikes and if they get a bit temperamental, well…"

George was on the verge of replying when everybody felt, through the soles of their feet, and then through the seats of their trousers, a rumbly sort-of vibration, which started to rattle their teeth before it rapidly became a loud noise, punctuated with squeaks and creaks.

"This contraption," said Bert, indicating the wooden cylinder, "is the 'Dynamic Drill' – we usually call it just DD – and these two fellows are explorers… of a sort."

Suddenly, a few yards away from the fireplace, a metal corkscrewy-thing, about six or seven feet in diameter, appeared from the ground, attached to what looked like a wooden cylinder with a conveyor belt underneath, mounted on wheels. When whatever it was became level with the ground, the corkscrew stopped turning, something which looked suspiciously like a submarine's periscope popped out of the roof, then swivelled around and stopped when it faced the three friends. Bert gave a resigned sigh and his shoulders drooped a little.

"Oh, rotten rhubarb," he said, to his surprised guests, who had no idea what was going on. "If you thought those Flugglebirds were pests, wait until you meet this pair!"

At that, a door opened in the rear of the contraption and out popped two men.

"What ho, what ho!" said the first fellow to appear, rather loudly. He was dressed in a green boiler suit, had large boots on his feet and stood about six feet tall. His wavy blond hair flopped over his forehead and he fixed the diners with watery blue eyes.

"C'mon, Bert," he said. "Aren't you going to intwoduce us to these guests?"

Bert looked rather pained but he announced to George and Tucklebinnie that they had the pleasure of meeting Roger Cholmondeley (pronounced Chumley) Carruthers-ffinch - but known to everyone as 'Carruthers'. His companion, a man of about the same height but dressed in a short-sleeved khaki shirt and long khaki shorts, topped with a solar topee above a luxuriant handlebar moustache, was introduced as Felix Montague Fortescue-Smythe, usually called 'Smythe' (pronounced Smith).

"This contraption," said Bert, indicating the wooden cylinder, "is 'The Dynamic Drill' - we usually just call it DD - and these two fellows are explorers... of a sort."

He continued, wearily, "Come on, you two, I expect you're hungry... as usual. Join us for a late supper and I'll try to explain what you do."

"Jolly good, jolly good," said Smythe. "One does work up quite an appetite pedalling that *boring* machine. 'Hwa, Hwa'" he chortled, pleased with his pun.

When everyone was seated and depleting Bert's provisions, Bert took a gulp of beer and said, "Right, let's see if I can describe why the DD was built and, probably more to the point, what it's doing here. Carruthers and Smythe realised a while ago that a lot of the world had been explored by people walking, or sailing, or using canoes. But, and this is the whole point of their argument, that meant that a lot was known about the surface, but not a lot was known about what was below the surface."

"That's right," said Carruthers. "I mean, it's all very well swanning about in jungles or deserts; anyone can do that, but it takes a special sort of person to go below the surface and see what's there."

Bert whispered to Tucklebinnie and George, "A lunatic, if you ask me."

Carruthers went on, "Smythe's dad is a jolly whizz-bang engineer, so we asked him if he could come up with some contwaption which would allow us to go from Point 'A' to Point 'B', without having to travel on the surface of the Earth. He thought about some sort of tunnelling engine and came up with 'The Dynamic Dwill'."

Tucklebinnie looked puzzled. Not only because Carruthers occasionally had trouble with the letters 'r' and 'w' which sometimes mixed themselves up for no good reason. "How does it work, then?" he asked.

"Ah-hah," said Smythe. "That's the cunning bit. Inside, there're some seats above pedals, which drive a big chain, attached to a gearbox. From the gearbox, the front of the machine rotates that sort-of corkscrewy drill thing which drives us forwards. We can tilt it a bit, to go up or down. The stuff it excavates passes under the DD on a conveyor belt-thingy and out the back into the hole that's just been created. The wheels are just to keep us rolling along and the whole thing is mounted on gimbals, like a compass, so we're always, well, almost always, the right way up. Need a bit more ballast, really."

"How'd you get it to go into the ground in the first place?" asked George, looking a bit puzzled.

"Well," said Carruthers. "That's all down to a lever at the back. We just pull it until the DD is facing into the ground, then we pedal like crazy. Best place to get started is the side of a hill, really, then when we are moving, we give us a bit of a tilt downwards and off we go. We've got a bit of equipment like a compass which always tells us where 'Up' is, so when we want to surface, it's just a matter of pedalling until we hit fwesh air and then we stop."

The conversation went on for some time but it became obvious that clever as it was, the DD suffered from one serious drawback. Navigation.

The intrepid explorers could plan where they wanted to go, but if the speed they were travelling was measured wrongly, or if the angle of travel was a tiny bit out, they could end up anywhere, really. And they did, quite frequently, according to Bert. Although, somehow, they always managed to return to somewhere near the 'Barn' when supplies were running a bit low!

Night was drawing in on the group gathered around the fire, so Bert suggested that it would be sensible to all get a good night's sleep, then they could have a chat in the morning and see if it might be possible to plan a bit of an adventure together. After all, what could possibly go wrong?

CHAPTER 4
An Adventure in the Offing

The following morning found the DD's pilots oiling chains, greasing wheels, and generally getting the machine ready for another expedition, while Tucklebinnie, George and Bert sat around the breakfast table, chatting about all sorts of things.

"Look," said Bert, eventually. "These two are quite good at what they do, even if they seem a bit batty, so I have a suggestion for a little trip. Come with me," he said, gesturing towards the workshop.

Lifting aside the dusty old sheet, Bert revealed a mass of copper and brass pipes all of which coiled round a big boiler. Above the boiler, but connected to it with a rather sturdy pipe was a smallish cylinder with a tap at one end.

Lifting aside the dusty old sheet, Bert revealed a mass of copper and brass pipes, all of which coiled around a big boiler. Above the boiler, but connected to it with a rather sturdy pipe, was a smallish cylinder with a tap at one end.

"This's my patented automatic treacle bender," he said, proudly. "You'll know, TeeBee, that bending raw treacle is a bit of a muscly job. Show the treacle too much light, or let it get too cold and you haven't a hope of getting any in (or out of) a can."

'My Uncle Humphrey had arms as thick as small tree trunks from wrestling with treacle in a tantrum.'

"Too true," said Tucklebinnie. "My Uncle Humphrey had arms as thick as small tree trunks from wrestling with treacle in a tantrum. He always said that it wasn't so much about having to bend the stuff, although that was what normally happened after a while. It was more like persuading the treacle that it actually wanted to be bent into a tin."

"Hang on," said George. "I know that treacle's found underground -

it's formed from ancient sugarcane forests, isn't it? 'S a bit like coal that used to be trees and ferns and things."

He went on, without waiting for an answer. "So how do we get treacle to the surface and why do we need to bend it? Isn't the raw stuff just a bit like thick toffee? We could just cut off a lump every now and then when we wanted to use it?"

Bert shook his head. "The really good treacle seams are quite deep down now and the dwarves think they own all of them, so we generally have to buy the stuff from a Treacle Merchant, who's bought it from a mining company."

He continued. "The problem is that the raw treacle, if it's soft, goes quite solid when it's exposed to light, and that's all we can buy. To get the hard stuff to go into cans or tins, it's got to be heated to just the right temperature, without too much light, and that's where my machine comes in. No guesswork needed, or messing about with great wodges of sticky stuff in darkness, just bung a lump or two in one end and nice soft treacle goes straight into a lovely tin at the other end. It's just that it can be difficult these days, to get good raw treacle."

Perhaps some explanation is needed. Dwarves are, by inclination, miners. However, they don't all mine the same things and they can be divided into three groups. The dwarves who mine gold, silver and diamonds tend to think they're the bees' knees and look down on the dwarves who mine iron, coal, or salt (dwarves don't mine pepper because it grows on trees!). They, in turn, look down on the Treacle Miners, who are getting pretty fed up with the whole business.

However, they all guard their mines fiercely and get pretty hot under the hard hat if anyone dares to suggest that perhaps other species could also do the work. The fact is that if you have a licence to mine, you can be any species you care to be. You can't steal from someone's mine, but if you happen to trip over a big nugget of gold when you're digging the garden, or a storm blows over a big tree in your back yard and exposes a treacle seam, then with the right licence, it's yours.

This perhaps explains why George was a bit troubled with speaking about treacle in public. Dwarves could be a bit of a handful if they thought someone else was mining whatever it was they were also mining. Or planning on mining.

"Anyway," said Bert. "The time before last that our two batty friends went off, they hit an uncharted treacle deposit. Lovely stuff it was, when they gave me a bit to try, and I could do with topping up my supplies before winter, so why don't we suggest they take you two along for a little treacle-trapping trip? I daresay they'd probably want to go a few other places as well, but with more legs to pedal than they normally have, it shouldn't take more than a couple of days."

"Is there room in that contraption?" asked Tucklebinnie. "I mean, George doesn't take up too much space, but I'm a bit bigger…"

"Actually," said Bert, "it's pretty well designed - bit like a yacht or a caravan, really - and it should be fine. There's a little kitchen, a couple of hammocks and a small loo, so it's quite self-contained. What d'you think? Shall we ask them?"

Tucklebinnie looked at George, and *vice-versa.*

"I'm always happy to have a go at something new," said Tucklebinnie. "In any case, I'm supposed to be a wizard, and we know that George can do a bit of magic from time to time, so I don't see any harm coming to us, provided we don't accidentally end up in a volcano. What d'you say, George?"

"I think I'd quite like a bit of an adventure. I'm a bit worried about the navigation, though. Are you going to come along, Bert?" he asked.

"It's probably better that I stay here," said Bert. "I've been on one or two trips in the past and anyway, I'll have to re-stock my pantry after I let you lot have enough food for even a short trip."

"Right," said Tucklebinnie, "let's see if our nutty navigator friends are happy to oblige."

"A tweacle twip, you say?" said Carruthers. "Sounds like jolly good fun, Smythe, old chap. Always good to have some pwime tweacle."

Smythe thought for a moment. "I daresay we can get to that undiscovered treacle - I've got all the measurements noted in my chart – and perhaps we can tack on a bit of a trip to the south Pointy Mountains. You know, those ones across the Noisy River where the slate quarries are supposed to be, although no-one's been there for years, since the giants moved in. We could use a couple of bits of slate."

There was a bit of a kerfuffle when the giants were mentioned, because very little was known about them except that they were big, and if you were a gnome, very, very big.

Tucklebinnie mentioned that the problem with giants, as he understood the matter, was not that they were in any way nasty; it was just that they had difficulty believing that there were small creatures who could talk amongst themselves. Half the time, the giants couldn't see who was making the funny squeaking noises anyway.

"It's a bit like us assuming that newts can't speak," said Tucklebinnie.

"Can they?" asked Carruthers.

"I don't know about all newts," said Tucklebinnie. "Isaac, the newt in my pond at home can - but perhaps that's just because there's a bit of leakage of spells from my house."

After more discussion, a rough plan was established and then the Dynamic Drill was stocked with supplies and equipment. This included a special 'dark safe' - a light-proof box in which raw treacle could be stored without problems until the return to Bert's Barn. Before the voyagers departed, Tucklebinnie gave Bert the pogo-stick as a 'thank-you' for his hospitality, but did warn him that he'd strengthened the spring with magic so that one bounce, then 'Spaaang' and Bert would find himself a good couple of hundred yards away from his starting point.

"S'not for just boinging about, Bert," said Tucklebinnie. "It's a genuine get-out-of-trouble bit of equipment, as used by the Imperial Guard down in Port 'na Storm. You might find it useful…"

"Thanks, TeeBee," said Bert, a bit doubtfully, not quite sure that he'd ever actually wanted a pogo-stick, but not wanting to appear ungrateful.

The intrepid voyagers climbed inside the Dynamic Drill; Bert made sure that all the hatches and doors were properly closed and then knocked on the outside four times, to tell everyone inside that they could get going. There were three seats above the chain drive, each

The four intrepid voyagers climbed inside the Dynamic Drill… George elected to sit at the navigator's table… Smythe operated the lever which tilted the DD… Carruthers counted 'one, two, three', the pedals were pushed and off they went.

with a set of pedals, so George elected to sit at the navigator's table while the three larger people made ready to depart. Smythe operated the lever which tilted the DD, then when the correct angle had been reached, which they could see by means of a big red metal arrow which always hung vertically and was fixed to the side, Carruthers counted, "One, two, thwee," the pedals were pushed and off they went. The DD disappeared into the ground, leaving behind a heap of earth, not unlike a rather large molehill.

Bert scratched his head in a thoughtful sort of way. "Well, let's hope they don't get too lost! Better get on, I suppose," he said. "Mushroom flans don't bake themselves and that lot will be rather peckish when they get back, I do believe."

CHAPTER 6
Treacly Trouble and Tricksters

Inside the Dynamic Drill, it was a bit noisy and a bit dim. The creaking of the chain, the whirring of the gearbox, the crunching of the drill-head and the *shlush-shlush* of the moving conveyor belt beneath their feet meant that the explorers had to shout a bit to be heard. There were some lights on the walls, powered by a small dynamo attached to the gearbox.

"How far to the treacle seam?" enquired Tucklebinnie.

"S'not so much a question of how far, more how many hours or days," said Smythe. "We measure everything in time here," he said, pointing to a big clock on one of the bulkheads. "The DD makes pretty much the same progress all the time, if we keep pedalling, so it's just a matter of making sure I keep the angles right. Anyway, I reckon it's about three hours to go before we hit the treacle."

"How do we actually know when we get to the treacle?" asked George. "I mean, we're burrowing through soil and rock here, so it's not like we know what's outside…"

"Ah ha," said Smythe. "But we do." He pointed to a glass pipe running along the inside of the wall of the Dynamic Drill. "As we move along, a bit of what we're drilling through gets pushed into the pipe so we can see what sort of stuff it is that we're travelling in. The inside of the pipe is super-slippy so nothing ever gets stuck."

"Chaps," called Carruthers from the front seat, after thirty minutes or so of pedalling. "D'you think someone could wustle up a cup of tea?"

George, doing not very much for the moment, was very happy to oblige and soon made himself at home in the kitchen - or 'galley' - as the sign said above the recessed alcove. It was almost gnome-sized and very well organised so he soon produced tea for all. He also discovered a packet of Bert's 'Super Fudge' cookies - treacle-based, of course - which he handed around (on a plate, naturally) to give the pedallers extra energy.

A couple of hours later, Smythe, in charge of navigation, did some quick calculations and said, "Carruthers, just pull the nose up a couple of stops on the lever, would you?"

Carruthers hauled on the metal handle until it clicked a couple of times, then asked, "How long, old chap, until the tweacle?"

"No more than ten minutes, if I've got my sums right," said Smythe. He had indeed got his sums right because a few minutes later, the glass pipe was filled with a black sludge.

"Up one more notch, Carruthers," said Smythe. "And one more minute's pedalling," he continued, speaking to Tucklebinnie and Carruthers.

The Dynamic Drill came to a stop and the pedallers eased their tired legs. George was quite excited.

"How do we get the treacle into the safe?" he asked.

"Hang on, hang on," said Carruthers. "Couple of things first. Because the tweacle's solidified from the sugarcane, it's left a bit of a space like a cave on top of the tweacle seam. No problem with breathing then, but if we try to cut some tweacle out, without special equipment, we could disappear in the soft stuff. Smythe's dad, good fellow that he is, invented some special shoes which let us get onto any soft tweacle that might be there without sinking. Then we move around until we find the best quality."

Carruthers produced a few pairs of 'treacle trainers' from the supplies store, a few hard hats with lamps attached and a large, sharp,

wedge-shaped spade, a 'V'- shaped thing that looked like the front end of a ship (the treacle plough) and a pair of heavy tongs with flat

ends. He also produced what looked like a toboggan, with a wide flat tray. "It's a bit like cutting peat," he said. "We have to make a bit of a trench with the

tweacle plough, then we cut tweacle into the trench using the spade and grasp it with the tongs. We put the slabs onto the sledge and then take them back to the Dynamic Dwill. The cut tweacle then goes into the safe."

He continued, "Smythe'll stay here and look after this end of the safety line and we'll do a bit of a recce. I'll go first with the safety line; George, you clip onto the line behind me and Tucklebinnie, you take up the rear, pulling the sledge if you would be so kind. Get the hats and boots on and let's go!"

They carefully loaded the sledge with the tools, found boots of the correct sizes, adjusted their cap-lamps, and then they were ready to 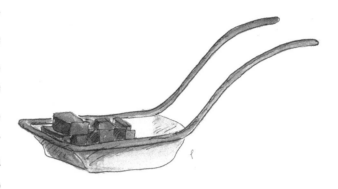 venture out onto the treacle. Tucklebinnie made sure that his robe of many pockets was firmly secured and not liable to drag - it's one thing to have a useful robe, it's quite another if it is permanently sticky.

Collecting the treacle was surprisingly easy because the Dynamic Drill seemed to have stopped very close to a section of the seam which was neither too sticky nor too soft, but what Carruthers claimed was, "Spiffing stuff." Handling the tools took a little practice, but very soon, the treacle safe was nearly full and the treacle cutting crew were on their last run, when, without any warning, lots of lights appeared in the cave, in a half-circle ahead of Carruthers.

"Drat and blast," said Carruthers, with feeling, and with his 'r's and 'w's behaving themselves for once. "Dwarves!"

"Smythe," he called out softly but with some urgency. "Get ready with Plan 'B' if we need to use it."

A sort-of gravelly voice spoke out of the darkness. "What have we here then, lads? Looks to me like we've got some illegal mining going on. Also looks like they're not even dwarves!"

Carruthers was caught in a beam of light aimed by the owner of the voice. "Explain what you're doing in our treacle," said the voice. "And it had better be a good explanation or the lads might get a bit restless."

"To whom should I address my weply?" asked Carruthers, in a steady voice, although the 'r's and 'w's had decided to have a tussle.

Carruthers was caught in a beam
of light aimed by the owner of the
voice. 'Explain what you're doing in
our treacle...'

"Seein' you're asking," said the voice, "I'm Jasper Rhyolite, Manager of Number 14 Treacle Crew, East Pointy Mountains Division. And who might you be?"

"Roger Carruthers, Chief Exploration Engineer, TeeBee and Gee Exploration Company," said Carruthers.

"So, I asks again, Mr. Chief Engineer, what're you doing in our treacle, and how'd you get here?" said Rhyolite. He obviously hadn't spotted the Dynamic Drill in the darkness.

"Well, Mister Manager, last time I checked, this area hadn't been claimed by anybody, so we just came for a look…"

"Everybody knows that only dwarves mine treacle, so it's ours, don't matter where it is," said Rhyolite, rudely and loudly.

Carruthers gave a cough and said, in a soft voice, "Plan B, Smythe, cast off," then continued in a much louder tone, "not sure that you are correct there, Mister Manager; other species can mine unclaimed tweacle if they have a licence. Anyway, we haven't broken any laws."

"We'll see about that," said Rhyolite. "You just get your gang together and get over here off the treacle and we'll ask our Senior Manager what's what."

"And if we don't?" asked Carruthers.

"Well, I don't generally like using force," said Rhyolite. "But we might just light up the cave, then the treacle'll go hard and you'll be stuck. Get yourselves over here," he said, pointing with his light to a spot a few tens of yards away.

Tucklebinnie whispered to George, "Time for your special bread, George; turn your lamp off, unclip yourself from the line and keep really quiet."

"Who's that?" queried Rhyolite, in the darkness.

'Time for your special bread, George ...'

"Just me," said Tucklebinnie. "The other half of Carruthers' team."

"Thought there was more than two of you," said Rhyolite.

"No, no," said Tucklebinnie. "I just put a couple of spare lamps around the place so we could see better, but they seem to be going out."

Meanwhile, Smythe had disengaged the safety line and was gently and quietly encouraging the Dynamic Drill into a submerged position, any noise being masked by the sucking noises Carruthers and Tucklebinnie made by deliberately stamping their boots. Smythe kept an eye on Carruthers through the periscope.

George, as has been mentioned, has some magical abilities, and one of his better spells goes into the making of a special bread. Just a mouthful or two makes the eater invisible for a couple of hours or so. He took some out of the pouch on his belt, swallowed most of a slice, and followed Carruthers to the spot to which Rhyolite had indicated they should make their way. Being much smaller and lighter than his two companions, his boots made very little impression on the surface of the treacle and, more importantly, no noise.

Once Tucklebinnie and Carruthers - and invisible George - had reached what proved to be a shelf of rock sticking out into the treacle, they were surrounded by dwarves and some more lamps were lit. As might be expected, the dwarves were stockily built, with powerful, if short, bodies and legs, not to mention muscular hands and arms, from all the digging, hacking and shovelling that was their life. Their faces were mostly hidden behind fierce-looking beards, topped off with hard-hats, to which lamps had been fixed.

"Right," said Rhyolite, looking at Tucklebinnie. "You look a bit wizardy, my friend, but don't try any tricks here. What's your name?"

"Really, Mr. Rhyolite," said Tucklebinnie. "You're being a bit rude, but if it pleases you to know, my name is Tucklebinnie and yes, I'm a wizard from a village a few hours' walk away to the east. Mr. Carruthers invited me to go exploring with him because I'm very interested in caves, rocks, and all manner of things which happen below the surface of the Earth, and he's an expert in these matters."

"Where's all your equipment then?" asked Rhyolite suspiciously.

"Oh, it's over there somewhere, near the cave entrance," said Tucklebinnie, waving vaguely behind him.

"No matter, no matter," said Rhyolite gruffly. "We'll pick it up later when we take you to the Senior Manager, Barytes Basalt, to see what he wants to do with you. Meanwhile, we've some treacle samples to collect. We're going to tie you up while we do that..."

"I say, I say," said Carruthers. "That's not cricket! I mean, it looks to me like you are exploring too, so it's not as if we are twespassing in your mine. We have as much right as you to be here."

"Perhaps, perhaps," said Rhyolite. "But there's me, Cinnabar Quartzite, Galena Granite, Pyrites Dolerite, Malachite Mudstone, Beryl Porphyry and Alabaster Arenite what says you two are getting tied up; I do believe we might just outnumber you. Do it," he snarled to his hench-dwarves.

They were made to sit back-to-back, to create an extra problem if they tried to escape, then tied up with some climbing rope produced by one of the dwarves. As all this was going on, George made sure he was out of anyone's way and although he couldn't be seen, he stayed just out of the light given off by the various lamps.

They were made to sit back-to-back ... then tied up with some climbing rope produced by one of the dwarves.

The dwarves headed off onto the treacle, testing bits of the seam with drills and hammers as they went, leaving Carruthers and Tucklebinnie looking rather forlorn in the meagre light of their cap lamps.

"Right, George," said Tucklebinnie, very quietly. "Would you please just cut these ropes? Carruthers, how do we signal Smythe?"

"No problem, old boy," said Carruthers. "He's watching us through the periscope. When the dwarves are on the other side of the cave, he'll surface, then we can creep back into the Dynamic Dwill and get out of this place. We'll leave our lamps here so it looks like we're still tied up, although the dwarves probably don't think we can possibly escape, in any case."

And that's exactly what they did, quietly gathering up their tools before slipping silently back into the Dynamic Drill which then

Quietly gathering up their tools
before slipping silently back into
the Dynamic Drill

submerged again. They did have a little bit of fun watching, through the periscope, the dwarves returning to the cap lamps and finding no prisoners. Tucklebinnie thought that he might have learned a few new words echoing through the walls of the Dynamic Drill, although he wasn't sure they could ever be used in polite company. Certainly not if his mum was listening.

"Down periscope," said Carruthers, quietly. "Gently does it chaps, but let's get those pedals moving and get out of here."

CHAPTER 6
Giants' playground

"Chaps," said Smythe, once they had resumed a steady pedalling rhythm. "It's not too far to the south side of the Pointy Mountains and the slate quarries there. We could surface for the night near the river - assuming this clock hasn't stopped it's just coming up to suppertime - get a bit of fresh air into the old DD, and have some grub around a camp fire. How does that sound?"

"Sounds very good to me," said George. "I'm only little, I know, but that means I need to eat more often than you bigger fellows and anyway, being nearly captured by those rude dwarves has given me quite an appetite. Just not for treacle!"

Smythe juggled his calculator, gave a few instructions and no more than fifteen minutes later, the nose of the Dynamic Drill encountered fresh air so they stopped pedalling and let the machine settle on its wheels. The adventurous explorers opened the rear door and looked around. They had surfaced in rather a pleasant little spot near a small river, with a few big oak trees about fifty yards back from the water. There were plenty of branches lying on the ground, so Tucklebinnie and Smythe went down to the river and brought back some large flattish stones with which they made a circular fireplace. George and Carruthers carefully laid dry twigs in the centre of the circle, and then popped a few bigger branches on top.

"Stand back," said Tucklebinnie, flexing his fingers in front of his face. "I haven't done this for a while, but let's see if I can get a fire going." He uttered a few magic words.

There was a bit of a 'whoosh', followed by, "Ow, ow, ow," as

Tucklebinnie sucked the ends of his fingers while, at the same time, he tried to put out a few bits of burning beard.

There was a bit of a 'whoosh', followed by "Ow, ow, ow" as Tucklebinnie sucked the ends of his fingers while, at the same time, he tried to put out a few bits of burning beard...

"Drat, I forgot how fast that spell works," he said, placing his singed fingers on his earlobes to remove the heat. (It's an old trick - try it sometime.) "I never seem to get my beard out of the way quick enough."

Meanwhile the twigs had caught alight and were burning well. George appointed himself 'Keeper of the Fire' (actually, no-one else minded) and busied around, making sure, before darkness fell, that there were enough branches to see them through the evening and placing one or two on the fire as the others began to burn down. Tucklebinnie fetched some deckchairs from the Dynamic Drill and arranged them around the fireplace.

Carruthers and Smythe raided the DD's stores, located some sausages which they carefully placed on sharp sticks angled towards the fire, popped a few potatoes and onions just inside the stone circle and handed around some of Bert's snacks as the sausages sizzled. Tucklebinnie placed a pot on a flat stone inside the circle and muttered to himself as he concocted something for pudding.

Soon, the explorers were busy eating supper (not bothering with plates, just using their fingers) and finishing off with Tucklebinnie's dessert speciality, hot chocolate with marshmallows, which he served in big mugs. George could just about have had a swim in his! But he didn't complain.

They couldn't stop talking about the day's adventures as they relaxed in their chairs.

"Dwarves," said Carruthers. "Short-tempered types, I've always thought. Too much bashing wocks and not enough sunlight can't be good for the disposition."

"I agwee, I mean, I agree," said Tucklebinnie, whose own 'w's and 'r's had a momentary lapse of concentration. "I've had dealings with them quite a few times now and getting new ideas into their heads is quite exasperating. There's their way of seeing the world, and the wrong way, as far as they're concerned. Oh well, we've got some treacle for Bert, so it's a happy end to a long day - what d'you think, chaps?"

He found he was speaking mostly to himself, since his spoken thoughts were met with snorting and snurkling noises as his fellow explorers succumbed to the effects of the day's efforts, coupled with both the toasty warmth of the fire and a filling meal.

"Oh well," he said to himself. "I'll use one of those hammocks in the Dynamic Drill - at least one of us won't have a sore neck in the morning!"

The next day began sunny and warm, so after washing their faces in the stream and generally getting at least a bit clean, the team had a

Tucklebinnie found he was speaking mostly to himself... as his fellow explorers succumbed to the effects of the day's efforts...

Boldy

decent breakfast of (to be honest, slightly rhubarb-flavoured) muesli, toast and tea. Fortunately, Tucklebinnie's toothpaste saved the day - the normal tube had mysteriously gone missing from the DD's bathroom - and, with gnashers cleaned, hair, beards and moustaches combed and brushed, the intrepid explorers set off once again. Not before, however, tidying up the overnight campsite - leaving only their footprints behind.

"Right," said Smythe. "If we go down at the proper angle for about ten minutes, then level out, we'll be under the Noisy River and I expect we should be at the quarries about lunch-time. I'd really like to collect a few bits of slate to give us extra ballast - and to put under teacups so they don't mark the galley table!"

A few hours of effort later - George was very happy to be able to help with some magically adapted pedals - the DD creaked into the open air and settled on a slight downward slope. Carruthers applied the handbrake. A quick look with the periscope didn't suggest anything problematic, so the rear door was opened and out hopped the mildly weary expedition members. It seemed as if they had indeed reached the southern Pointy Mountains. The view from their location showed they were about a third of the way up one of the peaks, looking east down into a broad valley, with a loop of the Noisy River in the blue-grey middle distance.

"I say," said Smythe. "Not a bad bit of navigation, if I say so m'self."

"Top-hole, old bean," said Carruthers. "Where d'you think these slate quarries are then?" he asked.

"I'd say…" began Smythe, whose answer was cut off by a very strident whirring sound, accompanied by a fast-moving shadow which disappeared eastwards. "I'd say…" he started again, only to be interrupted in the same fashion.

Tucklebinnie broke in. "I'd say the quarries are behind us and a bit higher up the mountain."

"Why'd you think that?" asked Carruthers, as another noisy shadow passed quickly overhead.

Tucklebinnie gently steered Carruthers around by his shoulders. "Look up there," he said, pointing to what looked like a pile of pancakes heaped up on a flattish bit of the mountain. "Wait a second and I think what you'll see is a giant picking up one of those slabs of rock. At a guess, I'd say they're moving slate by throwing bits of it about like we'd skip stones on a lake."

"Ah-ha," exclaimed Carruthers. "Whoever's throwing wock is definitely giant-sized," he said, his words drowned out by a whirring sound.

"And there's another," said Tucklebinnie, looking down slope as the whirring slab of rock was plucked out of the sky by what looked like - even at this considerable distance - a very large hand which then added the slab to a collection of pieces of slate.

The explorers decided just to sit tight for a while until the slate throwing had stopped, so the industrious George nipped back into the

DD and reappeared after a few minutes with tea and sticky buns for everyone.

"By George, that's welcome…" began Smythe, then convulsed into giggles. "Sorry, I didn't mean that badly, George, for you are quite one of the handiest fellows I've ever come across. Thank you for looking after us so well."

"S'all right, Smythe," said George, graciously. "We gnomes know we're only little, but it doesn't stop us from being useful members of society. Or expeditions, come to that."

After about twenty minutes or so, the whirring activity seemed to have ceased, so Tucklebinnie proposed that they try to contact the giants. "Problem is," he said, "because they're so big, their ears can't hear us properly; we sound like little squeaks when we talk. But, and this is a big but, we wizards have a secret which will sort that problem out. I'll show you, but you must keep quiet about it. Agreed?"

"Agreed," came the chorus of three.

Tucklebinnie took off his pointy hat and straightened it out. Placing the sharp end, which had a little hole in it, to his lips, he spoke.

"Hello there, giants," he said, and a very deep, slowed-down version of his words boomed out over the valley. "We'd like to have a chat with you, if that's OK?"

Tucklebinnie quickly moved the pointy end to his ear as a noise like somebody gargling with gravel came from all around. Tucklebinnie repeated what was being said.

"Whoever is replying says they'd like to see who's talking," he said. "I'll just move up the slope a bit and, if I can find it," he continued, rummaging around in his pockets, "I'll wave my big red-spotted hanky." This turned out to be more like the size of a small pillowcase, but it did the trick because whoever had been throwing slate from up the mountain gave a wave of a very, very large hand.

Placing the sharp end of his hat to his lips, Tucklebinnie spoke. "Hello there, giants."

More thundery noise filled the valley as Tucklebinnie stuck the hat to his ear once again.

"He says his name is Ginormous Gerald McCarthy and for us to come up the slope to where he's working. Sounds quite pleased to hear us, actually."

"Perhaps we don't all need to go at once?" suggested George, clearly not too happy with the prospect of meeting such a large creature.

"Good thinking, that gnome," said Carruthers. "Probably best if one of us DD drivers stays behind, in case we need to have a wescue mission."

"I think the giants are likely to be friendly," said Tucklebinnie. "But it'll do no harm if we do leave someone behind. George, if you'd like to give me your hat a minute, I can do the old megaphone - earphone

A few words were muttered, some small stars ignited briefly, and George's hat now had at least two more uses than just keeping his head dry

spell so you can hear what they're saying for yourself."

George, remembering that he still had some special bread in his pouch and so could disappear with a moment's munching if he had to, handed his hat over to Tucklebinnie. A few words were muttered, some small stars ignited briefly, and George's hat now had at least two more uses than just keeping his head warm and dry.

After moving the DD into the shade of an overhanging bit of rock to keep its presence secret, the threesome of Tucklebinnie, George and Smythe walked up the hill towards the giant. Tucklebinnie arranged to signal Carruthers if all went well - a horizontal wave of the hanky - or if things went badly, to listen for an invisible George.

Ginormous Gerald was much, much, bigger than they'd imagined, meaning that it took a bit longer than they'd thought to reach him.

"Distance does strange things to objects far away," muttered Tucklebinnie to himself. "Must remember that."

As they neared the giant, Tucklebinnie waved his hanky again, and used his hat to say, "Look down here, Ginormous Gerald, and please, please just whisper, otherwise we'll all be a bit deaf."

Ginormous Gerald, at least two times as tall as the height that George's gnome-home chimneypot was from the ground, looked down and smiled.

"Hello," he whispered. "And who might you chaps be? We don't get to meet many other people around here - usually they run away when they see us."

Tucklebinnie used his hat once more to both listen and to answer, introducing his two friends and saying that another one would be along in a while, probably.

Gerald invited the explorers to sit down, slightly up the slope from where he sat down, so that they were all at roughly the same eye level. Gerald's clothes seemed to be made of some sort of canvas and were a grubby browny-grey in colour, possibly because of all the rock dust, but he had a bright red neckerchief wrapped around his throat. His boots - one of which would have made George a rather splendid boat - had metal studs on the soles and his hat was made of hard leather, probably to prevent accidents. He had the usual eyes, ears, nose and mouth, although very large by human standards and his twinkly blue eyes looked out from under some ferociously luxuriant eyebrows.

"What brings you here?" he asked.

George, using *his* hat started to reply, "The Dynam..." when Tucklebinnie cut in.

"Sorry, George, I think Gerald means *why* are we here?

"Well, Gerald, we're curious types," he continued. "I mean, we're curious about what happens in different parts of the land, who and what lives where, what do people do to earn a living… that sort of thing. For instance, Smythe is an explorer and a bit of an engineer, I'm a wizard who mainly fixes broken bits and pieces and brews beer and George here is a well-known vegetable grower."

After Gerald gave out a giant-yodel, a few minutes later, other giants appeared... 'Iceberg' Reg Ramsbottom, Hildegaard 'Himalaya' Svensson, Seamus 'Alpine' McAlpine and Cecily 'Slatechucker' Forbes...

Gerald thought for a bit, then said, very quietly, "I think you should meet my friends, too. We're in the business of quarrying slate - and other things - to send down to Port 'na Storm for roof-building and making nice smooth floors. Let me call them - better cover your ears!"

After Gerald gave out a giant-yodel, a few minutes later, other giants appeared from both up and down the mountain. They were introduced as 'Iceberg' Reg Ramsbottom, Hildegaard 'Himalaya' Svensson, Seamus 'Alpine' McAlpine and Cecily 'Slatechucker' Forbes and they were all tremendously excited to meet the explorers, but Gerald had to ask them to, "Just whisper, please."

They were all dressed in a similar fashion to Gerald, although each neckerchief was a different colour. "So we can see who's who when all the dust is flying about," said Reg. Cecily explained that they all worked in the quarry above where they were sitting, using hammers and chisels to split the slate up into manageable slabs. It was a noisy and quite dusty business and they had to watch out for large lumps of rock suddenly breaking free. Every so often they'd build up so much slate that they had to move it out of the quarry, and that's what the giants had been doing when the explorers arrived.

Smythe, borrowing George's hat to chat, asked Alpine, one of the smaller giants, "How d'you get the slate down to Port 'na Storm?"

"Ah," said Alpine. "Once we get what we call a 'load' of the slate to the bottom of the mountains by throwing it like you saw us do earlier, we all station ourselves between it and a jetty on the Noisy River. We just skim the slate to each other and build up a great big stockpile near to the jetty. S' quite a good game, really, to see who drops the fewest pieces… or the most! We've got an arrangement with one of the barges that goes up and down to Port 'na Storm, so, once the stockpile is big enough, we just load the barge and off it goes.

"Mind you," he said chuckling. "There's quite a few broken bits of slate around, because if we get old Iceberg laughing, he doesn't concentrate so well and drops the odd slab here and there."

About then, Tucklebinnie decided, after a chat to his two companions, that the atmosphere was so friendly that it was time to bring Carruthers into the gathering. Tucklebinnie excused himself, climbed up the hill a little way and waved his hanky once again. After some time, Carruthers wheezed into view and was introduced. Or, as he might have said, if the 'r's and 'w's were at war, again, 'intwoduced'.

The giants picked up the DD very easily and took it back to where a meal was being prepared by Alpine ... ... the oile

The giants were intrigued as to how the explorers had arrived, unseen, so some explanations were in order and eventually, Tucklebinnie took Reg and Hildegaard down to where the Dynamic Drill was hidden. The giants picked up the DD very easily and took it back to where a meal was being prepared by Alpine and Cecily in a rock-built kitchen near the pile of slate. One giant's portion of food would have fed all the explorers about four times over. There wasn't much point in offering any of Bert's snacks to the giants - they would have barely registered as a faint taste - but the explorers did find out that the giants were very fond of rhubarb, although it didn't grow in this part of the land.

"I'm sure I could persuade my cousin Bert to send you a few cart-loads every so often," said George, after swallowing a mouthful of cloudberry crumble and then using his magical hat to talk to Cecily. "Mind you, he'll want to be paid or to have something in return, so please have a think and let me know when you've decided. Mmmh, this cloudberry stuff is delicious!"

There was lots of conversation as the evening drew on, with much borrowing of hats, but eventually nearly everyone went off to find a comfortable place to sleep. Tucklebinnie and Smythe sat around the embers of the fire the giants had made, chatting about this, that and the other.

"I'd like to be able to get some ballast for the DD from the broken slabs before we leave," said Smythe. He went on, "We could ask if a couple of the giants could carry the DD to the jetty on the Noisy River - it would save us most of a day's pedalling - then we'd be able to get back to Bert's quite quickly. I think this notion of George's of trading the occasional bit of rhubarb for a few lumps of rock could let Bert branch out a bit in business. It's not as if rhubarb grows all year around. What d'you think, TeeBee?"

"I think it's a good idea, but perhaps we should suggest that just one or two of the giants come with us to Bert's - I mean, it's not as if the Noisy River is any problem to them - and we can do the introductions and so on?"

"Let's sleep on it, then," said Smythe. "'Night, TeeBee, see you bright and early."

CHAPTER 7
Back to Bert's

The next morning, after breakfast, Tucklebinnie and George excused themselves for a few minutes for a chat, while the DD drivers checked the sprockets, kicked the tyres, oiled and greased the oily and greasy bits and had a good scout around for potential ballast. The giants had left early to finish off the load of slate they were preparing to send to the stockpile at the jetty.

"These giants are really nice, aren't they, Tucklebinnie?" asked George, sitting himself down on a large tussock of grass.

"I do believe you're absolutely right, George," said Tucklebinnie. "It seems as if a lot of people are afraid of them, just 'cos they're so big, but they seem to work hard and it looks like they've a good business going here. I actually think that they might just be a little bit lonely.

"Listen," he went on. "That idea of yours about Bert exchanging rhubarb for rock - d'you really think Bert would be up for a bit of occasional trade?"

"Well," said George, "Bert's only a rhubarjack for less than three months of every year at best and the brassica business doesn't take a lot of time, so he's always looking for work in the off-season. You've seen how ramshackle his barn is but if he could build something a bit sturdier, he could have a better store for the treacle and the rhubarb. With enough slate, he could probably open a proper business like 'Bert's Building Supplies' or something similar. He could sell or trade the stuff to other people who want to build nice houses or stores."

"That's what Smythe thought," said Tucklebinnie. "Let's see if

Ginormous Gerald is keen, and if he is, then we can chat to Bert and find out what he thinks."

With that, he explained to Carruthers and Smythe the Grand Plan. Luckily, when Ginormous Gerald returned, he also thought it could be a good arrangement, so not only was the slate load to be finished, but the DD would also be carried to the jetty when everyone was ready. Afterwards, perhaps a couple of the giants would accompany Tucklebinnie and George to Bert's Barn where the rhubarb-rock exchange could be discussed. Meanwhile, the giants had found some pieces of slate for ballast, and trimmed them down a bit to fit the shape of the DD. Carruthers and Smythe did a quick test-bore and pronounced that the addition of the ballast was 'absolutely top-hole!'

The business of getting the slate to the jetty began with the slate-skimming giants taking up their allotted positions, then moving the load for quite a distance, before doing the whole thing over again… And again, until they reached the river.

"Getting a large flat bit of slate landing on your hat wouldn't be too

The business of getting the slate to the jetty began with the slate-skimming giants taking their allotted positions…

much fun," said Smythe, to which everyone nodded agreement, the explorers walking leisurely along the track but keeping well behind the giants as they moved ever closer towards the Noisy River. Gerald had said that the DD would be picked up last, once the moving of the slate had been completed.

Later the same day as the sun was getting low in the sky, part of the river jetty was covered with a full load of slate piled up, waiting for a barge. A ragtag assembly of giants, humans and a magical gnome sat on the riverbank, looking at dragonflies swooping over the reed-beds which covered the shallow parts of the riverbed. A carefully carried Dynamic Drill had been placed near, but not too near, to the river's edge. The barge was due the following day, so it was agreed that everyone would camp for the night, the giants would load the barge when it arrived, and then the second part of the plan would begin.

The Noisy River was quite wide at this point, which is why the jetty had been built. The width of the river not only allowed other traffic on the river to keep on going while a barge was being loaded or unloaded, it also allowed large water-craft to turn around with ease. There was a much smaller jetty on the north side - just large enough to allow a little ferry somewhere to dock when people needed to get from one side to the other.

The next morning, after the river mist had cleared, it was obvious to everyone on the south side that there was a traveller on the north side who was quite anxious to cross. What gave the game away was the

It was obvious to everyone on the south side that there was a traveller on the north side who was quite anxious to cross. What gave the game away was the 'boooiiinngg, booiiinngg' noise he made when leaping up to try and attract the attention of Walter the Boatman . . .

'boooiiinngg, boooiiinngg' noise he made when leaping up to try to attract the attention of Walter the Boatman, the owner of the ferry, who had joined the giants and the explorers for a cup of tea while waiting for the barge to bring him some supplies he'd ordered. It was Bert, who had obviously been practising getting around on his pogo-stick.

Rather than ask Ginormous Gerald to just stride across the river and pick Bert up, which might have given Bert rather a rude shock, Walter made a quick trip and returned, complete with the excited gnome (and his pogo-stick). Walter had explained about the giants on the journey back, so Bert wasn't too surprised at their size but was very glad when Tucklebinnie magicked Bert's hat so that he could understand what they said. Bert explained that he'd had an unexpected message that Bluebell would be coming back from Port 'na Storm by barge, so he'd used the pogo-stick to travel down to the river to meet her rather more swiftly than he'd have managed just by walking.

George and Tucklebinnie made their excuses and took Bert aside, after the introductions had been made, to explain to him the possible business proposition. Would he be interested? Bert thought for a while.

"So," he said, "these giants are fond of a bit of rhubarb then. I do need to rebuild the 'Barn', that's for sure, and perhaps if I put a bit of thought in, perhaps it could become a trading post sort-of-thing. I mean," he said, blushing, "if Bluebell and I get married we could have 'Bert and Bluebell's Barn' or something like that, anyway. Yes, I'm happy to trade a bit of rhubarb for some stone. Mind you, what I think is a 'bit' might not be the same as what Ginormous Gerald thinks, but there's plenty of room for discussion. And plenty of rhubarb - it's gone a bit mad these last couple of years and there's only so much that can be kept. Far better that it gets used."

With that, Tucklebinnie called Ginormous Gerald over - his name had been shortened to his initials for ease of conversation - and in the space of a few sentences, a deal was done. It wasn't exactly possible for Bert and GG to shake hands, given that Bert could comfortably stand in one of Gerald's, but each was comfortable with the other's spoken word.

It wasn't exactly possible for Bert and Ginormous Gerald to shake hands, given that Bert could comfortably stand in one

"I reckon three weeks on Wednesday should see the first of the main crop of rhubarb ripe," said Bert. "I'll probably need two days or so to get the stuff lopped and carted back to the 'Barn', so how about meeting up on the following Saturday?

"Probably easiest if we meet near, but not too near, my house," continued Bert to Gerald, giving him directions. "If you're going to skim some slate, best that there's no chance of any accidents giving me or my neighbours a fright. I'll have a stack or two ready for you nearby and we can see how things work out."

Gerald thought that this was a sound idea, but said that on this first visit, he'd probably just come alone and bring a big sackful of slate until they'd worked out a good plan.

"Perhaps I could stay over and meet some of your neighbours?" suggested Gerald. "That way, they won't be surprised when they see us about on the odd occasion."

"Excellent idea," said Bert. "I'll be sure to get some BIG pies baked before you come."

When the barge arrived, Bluebell was indeed aboard

Puddy

When the barge arrived, Bluebell was indeed aboard and, after the conversation side of things was sorted out, was quite delighted to meet all the new people.

It didn't take too long for the slate to be loaded, then Ginormous Gerald and Hildegaard carried the DD over the river and Walter ferried the human and gnome cargo - and their various rucksacks - across. After all the goodbyes had been said, the giants left for their quarries and the others headed for Bert's Barn, a couple of hours away at a normal walking pace, or at about the same speed as the DD, travelling on a parallel course but underground, naturally.

George was keen to chat away to Bert and Bluebell, leaving Tucklebinnie to stroll along, quite happily, thinking all sorts of wizardly thoughts. *Must speak to Bert about rhubarb wine; I'll have to invent a better way for people of different species to speak to each other - perhaps I should ask Isaac? I wonder how that new treacle tastes? Mustn't forget the FluggleTrap; what's for lunch? Why did I pack the goblin declogger? Such are the minds of wizards!*

George was keen to chat away to Bert and Bluebell, leaving Tucklebinnie to stroll along quite happily, thinking wizardly thoughts.

After the Dynamic Drill had arrived at the 'Barn', it was time to use the Treacle-Bender to transfer the treacle from the safe to some shiny new tins which Bluebell had thoughtfully acquired on her trip to Port 'na Storm. Bert fired up the boiler and in the semi-dark caused by a thick canvas sheet over everything, opened the treacle safe. The treacle hadn't suffered from being transported and went quite happily into the Bender from where it emerged a few minutes later, almost as a runny liquid, from the tap at the top into the tins waiting below. It was obvious, on a first taste-test that it was

It was quite obvious, on a first taste test, that it was indeed of 'pwime quality'

indeed of 'pwime quality'.

Bert presented the DD crew with a few smaller tins to re-stock the store cupboard; Tucklebinnie and George were each given a large tin with 'Only to be opened in a dark place' firmly printed on the labels and then it was time for supper, to celebrate a short but eventful expedition, and Bluebell's safe return. A few neighbours were invited, including Bluebell's parents, and the evening soon passed by in a haze of good food, very acceptable beer (for those that wanted it, mainly

Carruthers, Smythe and Tucklebinnie), songs and chat. When the visitors began to leave, Tucklebinnie used a magic spell to help tidy up the 'Barn' - burning his beard only very slightly - and everyone headed off for a night's rest.

The next morning, George was anxious to set off home to see if the patching-up of his vegetable garden had worked after the Flugglebird damage, so he and Tucklebinnie loaded up the FluggleTrap. Not before, however, instructing Bert in the best way to sow and look after the purple carrot seeds and accepting a small bundle of early season rhubarb, "For a nice bit of pudding when you get home!"

Tucklebinnie and George set off in the cool mid-morning, waving as they went.

The slightly batty DD drivers decided to pootle around for a bit, helping Bert for a few days, while they planned their next big trip. "You never know," said Carruthers. "Might just pop in to see you George, one of these days…"

"You're welcome anytime," said George. "But please, don't make a hole in my vegetable garden. It's bad enough having slugs, snails and Flugglebirds but I don't need any bigger pests! In any case, you'd probably give the local moles an inferiority complex."

Tucklebinnie and George set off in the cool of the mid-morning, waving as they went, Tucklebinnie pushing the by-now-much-lighter FluggleTrap. Well, without two rather carrot-filled fowl, it would be, wouldn't it?

A couple of weeks later, Bert received a somewhat tatty postcard.

It read: 'Hello Bert, just to let you know that George and I are fine - not sure when we'll be home though - things have taken a slightly odd turn…' It was signed, TB, but it was difficult, if not impossible, to see the postmark.

Oh well, thought Bert. *I'm sure they'll be all right, after all Tucklebinnie IS a wizard. Isn't he?*

To Be Continued

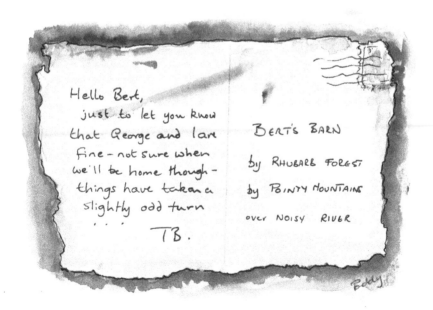